JOURNEY OF THE GREAT LAKE

LAND OF THE DINGO PEOPLE

BY PERCY TREZISE

Angus&Robertson
An imprint of HarperCollins*Publishers*

This saga, JOURNEY OF THE GREAT LAKE, is dedicated to my colleague of many years, Aboriginal author and artist Dick Roughsey. It is also dedicated to all my Aboriginal friends who led me through their temples of Dreamtime, passing on the legends and stories of their race memory, which records their history back through countless millennia, recalling the dramatic humid and arid weather phases of the Ice Age.

The saga is set circa 30,000 years ago to encompass the extinct megafauna of marsupials, reptiles and birds, the giants of Dreamtime, which shared this ancient land with the people of those times.

Percy Trezise

Angus&Robertson
An imprint of HarperCollins*Publishers,* Australia

First published in Australia in 1997
by HarperCollins*Publishers* Pty Limited
ACN 009 913 517
A member of the HarperCollins*Publishers* (Australia) Pty Limited Group

Copyright © Percy Trezise 1997

HarperCollins*Publishers*
25 Ryde Road, Pymble, Sydney, NSW 2073, Australia
31 View Road, Glenfield, Auckland 10, New Zealand
77–85 Fulham Palace Road, London W6 8JB, United Kingdom
Hazelton Lanes, 55 Avenue Road, Suite 2900, Toronto, Ontario M5R 3L2
and 1995 Markham Road, Scarborough, Ontario M1B 5M8, Canada
10 East 53rd Street, New York NY 10032, USA

National Library of Australia Cataloguing-in-Publication data:

Trezise, Percy.
Land of the Dingo people.
ISBN 0 207 19091 7.

1. Aborigines, Australian – Legends – Juvenile literature.
I. Title.
398.20994

Printed in Hong Kong

9 8 7 6 5 4 3 2 1   97 98 99

INTRODUCTION

Aboriginal oral history tells of hundreds of Dream Roads criss-crossing
the Australian continent which were made by Ancestral Beings during
their travels at the beginning of Dreamtime. It also tells of a vast freshwater lake
at the top of Australia and the Anta Moola sisters who travelled down the west side
of this lake distributing waterlilies and unborn human baby spirits.

There is scientific evidence to suggest that 36,000 years ago there was a large freshwater lake
at the top of Australia. Scientists called it the Lake of Carpentaria . . .
and it was also known as Balanorga, the big water.

This is the story of three children's journey around Balanorga and along
the Dream Road of the Anta Moola sisters to find their way home.

Percy Trezise
Cairns, Queensland
1997

Jadianta, Lande and Jalmor were far from their home and clan, the Kadimakara People. They were cold, stiff and desperately hungry but they had survived the great storm and long journey across the big water, Balanorga.

The rising sun began to warm the children as they waded ashore. There were no bark *gunyahs* or other signs of life among the paperbark trees fringing the lake. Then a dingo howled and Jadianta, Lande and Jalmor saw a yellow dog watching them from the top of a low rise.

Jadianta started to lead Lande and Jalmor towards the dingo knowing it would lead them to people, hopefully friendly people. Suddenly, the yellow dog was surrounded by a group of children, silently watching.

The watching children saw the battered *walpa* and realised the sorry plight of its three passengers. They came running towards them, smiling and calling out in a strange language which the Kadimakara children could not understand.

Jadianta had learned finger talk. He gestured that they were starving and needed food. He said, '*Minya, minya*', which means meat. The surrounding children laughed and, gesturing towards their own camp, said, '*Minya, minya.*'

As they walked up the rise together, the welcoming children signed that they were the clan of the Dingo People. Jadianta signed that they were from the Kadimakara People on the far side of Balanorga and blown by the great storm across the lake.

From the top of the rise Jadianta, Lande and Jalmor saw a cluster of *gunyahs* among trees and by the creek *walpas* were moored. Smoke was rising from cooking fires and ground ovens, and people were preparing to go hunting. It was just like their home with the Kadimakara People and Jadianta, Lande and Jalmor happily followed the Dingo children.

The ground ovens were opened and Jadianta, Lande and Jalmor were soon eating steaming barramundi and turtle, and roasted waterlily bulbs. The Dingo People gathered around to see the castaways from a distant land.

In the kinship system all clans were divided into two halves named black cockatoo and white cockatoo. Jadianta indicated they were black cockatoo and an old man signalled which of the surrounding people were their brothers, sisters, cousins, aunts, uncles, parents and grandparents in the kinship system.

When the children finished eating, a man, Bunbudji, sat down with them and spoke. To their surprise he spoke their language. 'I stand as your mother's brother and so must help you all I can. What do you want to do?'

Jadianta said, 'We want to get back home. We can't paddle back so we will have to walk around Balanorga. Which way should we go?'

Bunbudji said, 'I travelled much as a young man, visiting relatives.' He drew a map of the lake on the ground and said, 'You cannot go north, though that is the shortest way. Up there lies the jungle land of the headhunters who will kill you.'

Bunbudji pointed his chin south. 'You must go south but it is a very long way. You must follow in the footsteps of our ancestors, the Anta Moola sisters, who travelled that way in Dreamtime, filling the lagoons with waterlilies of all colours to provide food for people.'

The People of the Dingo believed that the Anta Moola sisters left all the human baby spirits in the lagoons for future generations — in the mud. They believed the old women, the Kweelucs, now curlew birds, looked after those baby spirits so they couldn't wander off and get lost.

Then Bunbudji told Jadianta, Lande and Jalmor the story of the sisters and the Dream Road they had made around Balanorga.

'When those girls, Marbee and Nardoo, the Anta Moola sisters, had finished with the waterlily and baby spirit business they travelled east around the great lake towards the islands, the home of their future husbands, the Lizard brothers. Soon they found they were being followed by that greedy man, Gidja the Moon, who wanted the Anta Moola sisters for his wives. Gidja followed Marbee and Nardoo until, finally, he caught them.

'The Anta Moola sisters didn't like Gidja. They decided to trick him and escape. Marbee told Gidja that she and Nardoo would dance for him. As they danced, the magic sisters were surrounded by campfire smoke then they changed into dancing brolgas and flew away.

'Marbee and Nardoo had a long journey and along the way they had created many places. Finally they reached the coast and sat down on a mountain looking out to the islands of the sunrise. They were waiting for their future husbands, the Lizard brothers.

'I saw those sisters, Marbee and Nardoo, a long time ago. They were sitting up there among the clouds, still waiting for those Lizard boys. The two sisters waited so long, they turned into stone on top of that mountain.'

Bunbudji told the Kadimakara children the story of the Anta Moola sisters so they would know how to follow their Dream Road around Balanorga but encouraged the children to stay with the Dingo People while they prepared for their long journey.

The three children felt very much at home as in the Land of the Dingo People everybody called them by their relationship to them whether brother, sister, cousin, son or daughter. With the help of sign language, it wasn't long before the children of the Kadimakara People soon understood the children of the Dingo People.

Their new-found relatives helped Jadianta, Lande and Jalmor build a bark *gunyah*, then gather materials to make fish-spears, nets, fishing-lines, digging sticks and everything else they would need for their long journey home. Bunbudji even gave Lande a young dingo. 'Her name is Lasca. She will always look after you and warn you of any danger,' he said.

A full moon cycle passed while Jadianta, Lande and Jalmor made the implements for hunting and fishing like fire-sticks, stone knives and dillybags to carry them in. They each had a roll of softened paperbark for sleeping blankets.

At last the children were ready for their journey home. Bunbudji said, 'I have sent up smoke to let the People of the Magpie Goose know that you three children are coming. They will let you cross their country, following the footsteps of the Anta Moola sisters.'

It was time to go. The older Dingo children went with Jadianta, Lande and Jalmor to the Moon River, where their land ended. They showed them some *walpas* moored at the bank for the Kadimakara children to use to cross the river.

One of the older boys, Moolbi, signed that he would help them paddle across and then bring the *walpa* back. The Kadimakara children placed their belongings and Lasca the dingo on the *walpa* and pushed off, waving bark paddles in farewell to the Dingo children.

The river was fairly wide but there was hardly any current so it was easy to paddle. Moolbi pointed out places on the far bank where tall reeds had been chopped out to clear landing places; *walpas* were moored there but there were no people.

They were paddling past the reeds when Lasca snarled. Suddenly, there was a huge splash as a giant crocodile launched itself out of the reeds and seized the boy, Moolbi, in its jaws. The crocodile ripped Moolbi off the *walpa*, Moolbi's flailing legs hit Jalmor and knocked him into the water as well.

Jadianta and Lande looked at the swirling water where Moolbi and Jalmor had disappeared. They could hear screaming and wailing coming across the water from the Dingo children.

Then Jalmor's head rose out of the water and he was seized by a sobbing Lande and hauled back on the *walpa*. Jadianta jumped into the shoulder-deep water and began desperately dragging the *walpa* to shore.

Jadianta reached the bank and they all grabbed their belongings and ran away from the water followed by Lasca.

Safe on top of the bank they turned and waved to the wailing Dingo children on the other side. They all knew there was no hope for poor Moolbi taken by the huge crocodile. Behind them voices were calling; people were coming to meet the three children and wondering why the distant Dingo children were crying and wailing.

Jadianta, Lande and Jalmor were no longer in the land of the friendly Dingo People — they were alone and in the land of the Magpie Goose People.

Jadianta, Lande and Jalmor and their dingo pup, Lasca, have to journey around the great lake, Balanorga, to find their way home. They will follow the Dream Road of their ancestors, the Anta Moola Sisters, and travel through the unknown *Land of the Magpie Goose, Land of the Emu People* and into the terrifying *Land of the Snake Men.*

The Kadimakara children's journey back to their home will be long and dangerous. Will they ever see their family again?

GLOSSARY

Ancestral Beings   people who came down from the stars at Creation Time and turned into every species of life on earth; animal and plant

Balanorga   the name for the great lake; bala=big, norga=water

black cockatoo / white cockatoo   the names of the two halves of the Aboriginal kinship system in these clans

Dream Road   the path of an Ancestral Being during Dreamtime

Dreamtime   the time of the creating of Ancestral Beings

finger talk   a sign language which is understood by many clans

gunyah   a circular hut covered with paperbark

kadimakara   a bullock-sized marsupial similar to a wombat

Kadimakara People   a clan on the east side of the lake

Kweelucs   old women of the lagoons who looked after human baby spirits during Dreamtime

walpa   a raft